Wee Sing®
SING-ALONGS

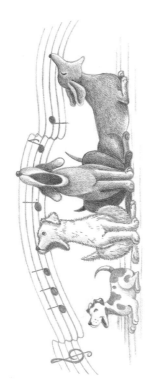

By
Pamela Conn Beall and
Susan Hagen Nipp

Illustrated by
Nancy Spence Klein

PSS!
PRICE STERN SLOAN

PREFACE

Singing along with family and friends is a joyful experience, whether in a small group or a large gathering. A kindred spirit and a warm fellowship are created by the blending of voices.

All kinds of wonderful songs can be sung together. The mood may be boisterous and happy, making you want to "Sing, Sing Together," as in the first section of the book. The next section of spirituals may fill the need to "Rocka My Soul" as the rhythmic songs lend themselves to expression through clapping, snapping, or tapping.

Voices blend together "Round 'n' Round," producing the sound of a wondrous choir as these simple yet challenging rounds of the third section are sung. Finally, when "Day Is Done" and the mood shifts to the quieter songs, the last section offers beautiful melodies that are lovely for harmonizing and a warm good-night.

Whether you sing around the campfire, in the car, or just at home, these are wonderful songs for sharing, expressing, shouting, enjoying. Music speaks to all of us and in this spirit we join you in song.

Pam Beall
Susan Nipp

4

Round 'n' Round

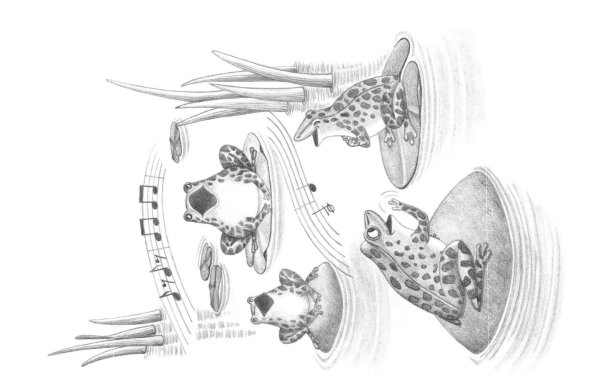

KOOKABURRA

Australia

1. Kook-a-bur-ra sits in the old gum tree,—

Mer-ry, mer-ry king of the bush is he,—

Laugh, Kook-a-bur-ra, laugh, Kook-a-bur-ra,

Gay your life must be.

2. Kookaburra sits in the old gum tree
Eating all the gumdrops he can see,
Stop, Kookaburra, stop, Kookaburra,
Leave some there for me.

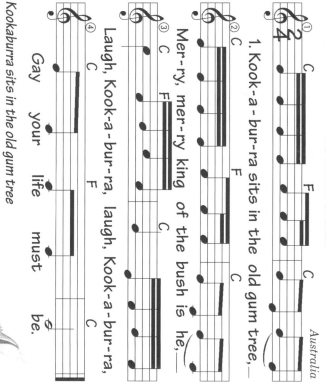

WHY SHOULDN'T MY GOOSE?

English

Why should-n't my goose Sing as well as thy goose

When I paid for my goose Twice as much as thou?

FROG ROUND

American

① D   ②

Hear the live-ly song of the frogs in yon-der

③

pond, Krik, krik, krik,   krik, krik, krik, krik,   brrr - um!   ④

WHITE CORAL BELLS

English

① A   E7   A   E7   A

1. White cor-al bells up - on a slen-der stalk,

② A   A7

Lil - ies of the val-ley deck my gar-den walk.

2. Oh, don't you wish that you could hear them ring?
That will happen only when the fairies sing.

7

SCOTLAND'S BURNING

English

① C7   F   C7   F   ② C7   F

Scot-land's burn-ing, Scot-land's burn-ing, Look out!

C7   F ③ C7   F   C7   F ④ C7   F

Look out! Fire! Fire! Fire! Fire! Pour on wa-ter, Pour on wa-ter.

LITTLE TOM TINKER

Traditional

① C

Lit - tle Tom Tink - er got burned by a ②

③   ④

clink - er And he be-gan to cry,

⑤   ⑥   ⑦   ⑧

"Ma,— Ma,— What a poor fel-low am I."

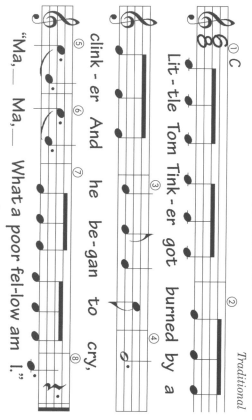

DOWN BY THE STATION

Traditional

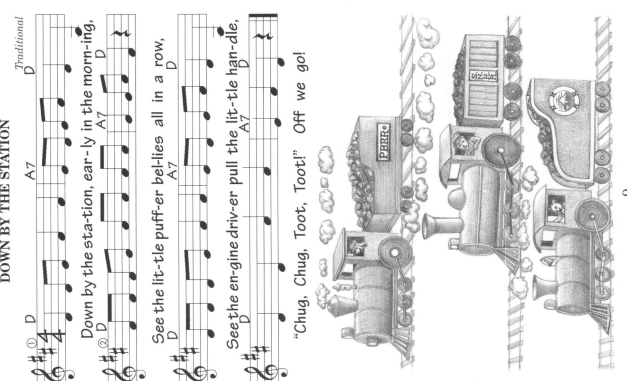

Down by the sta-tion, ear-ly in the morn-ing,

See the lit-tle puff-er bel-lies all in a row,

See the en-gine driv-er pull the lit-tle han-dle,

"Chug, Chug, Toot, Toot!" Off we go!

ARE YOU SLEEPING?
(Frère Jacques)

French

Are you sleep - ing, Are you sleep - ing, Broth-er John,
Fré - re Jac - ques, Fré - re Jac - ques, Dor-mez vous,

Broth - er John? Morn - ing bells are ring - ing,
Dor - mez vous? Son - nez les ma - ti - nes,

Morn - ing bells are ring-ing, Ding, ding, dong! Ding, ding,dong!
Son - nez les ma - ti - nes, Din, din, don! Din, din, don!

ROW, ROW, ROW YOUR BOAT

E. O. Lyte

Row, row, row your boat, Gent-ly down the stream,—

Mer-ri-ly, mer-ri-ly, mer-ri-ly, mer-ri-ly, Life is but a dream.—

THREE BLIND MICE

English, 1609

① C   G7   C   G7   C   ② G7   C

Three blind mice, Three blind mice, See how they run,

③ G7   C   G7   C

See how they run, They all ran af-ter the farm-er's wife, She

G7   C   G7   C

cut off their tails with a car - ving knife, Did you

④ G7   C   G7   C

e - ver see such a sight in your life as Three blind mice?

11

Suggestion:

Sing a round using *Row, Row, Row Your Boat* as Part 1, *Are You Sleeping?* as Part 2, and *Three Blind Mice* as Part 3.

REUBEN AND RACHEL

American, 1800s

① C   ②

1. Reu - ben, Reu - ben, I've been think - ing,

What a grand world this would be, If the boys were

all trans-port-ed Far be - yond the north - ern sea.

2. Rachel, Rachel, I've been thinking,
What a grand world this would be,
If the girls were all transported
Far beyond the northern sea.

SWEETLY SINGS THE DONKEY

English

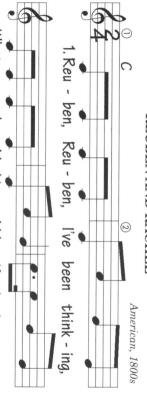

D   A7   D

Sweet - ly sings the don-key at the break of day;

A7   D

If you do not feed him, this is what he'll say:

D   A7   D

Hee - haw! Hee - haw! Hee-haw, hee-haw, hee-haw, hee-haw!

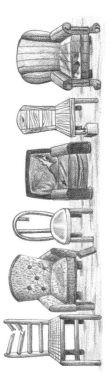

CHAIRS TO MEND

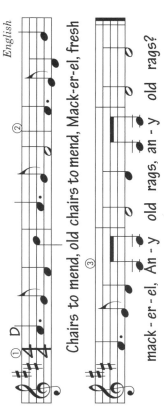

① D

Chairs to mend, old chairs to mend, Mack-er-el, fresh

mack - er - el, An - y old rags, an - y old rags?

A RAM SAM SAM

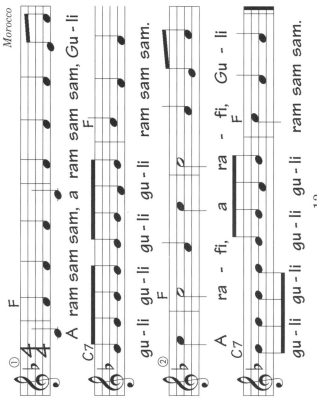

① F

C7

A ram sam sam, a ram sam sam, Gu - li

F

gu - li gu - li gu - li gu - li ram sam sam.

② F

A ra - fi, a ra - fi, Gu - li

C7 F

gu - li gu - li gu - li gu - li ram sam sam.

13

DONA NOBIS

Anonymous

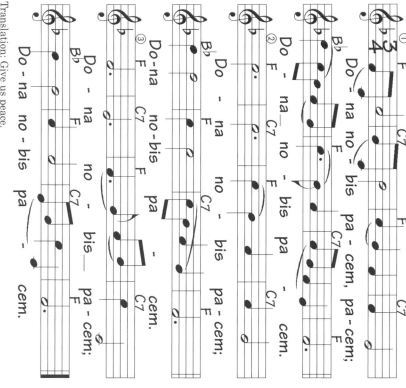

Do - na no - bis pa - cem, pa - cem;

Do - na_ no - bis pa - cem.

Do - na no - bis pa - cem;

Do - na no - bis pa - cem.

Do-na no-bis pa - cem.

Do - na no - bis pa - cem;

Translation: Give us peace.

FOR HEALTH AND STRENGTH

Traditional

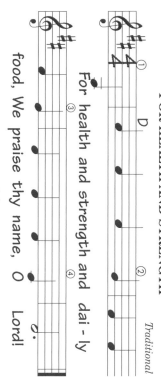

For health and strength and dai - ly food, We praise thy name, O Lord!

MAKE NEW FRIENDS

English

Make new friends but keep the old;— One is sil-ver and the oth-er gold.

COME, FOLLOW

John Hilton
1599–1657

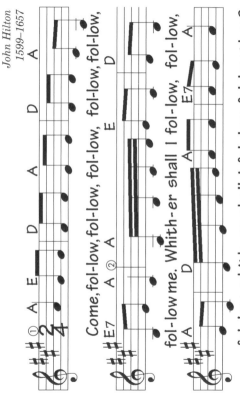

Come, fol-low, fol-low, fol-low, fol-low, fol-low me. Whith-er shall I fol-low, fol-low, fol-low, whith-er shall I fol-low, fol-low thee? To the green-wood, to the green-wood, to the green-wood, green-wood tree.

OH, HOW LOVELY

German, 1800s

① D   G   D   G   D
Oh, how love-ly is the eve-ning, is the eve-ning,

② D   G   D   G   D
When the bells are sweet-ly ring-ing, sweet-ly ring-ing,

③ D   G   D
Ding, dong, ding, dong, ding, dong!

SING TOGETHER

English

① F   C7   F
Sing, sing to-geth-er, mer-ri-ly, mer-ri-ly sing,

② C7   F
Sing, sing to-geth-er, mer-ri-ly, mer-ri-ly sing,

③ C7   F
Sing, sing, sing, sing, sing.

HEY, HO! NOBODY HOME

English, 1609

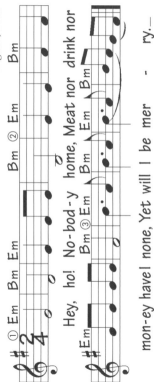

Hey, ho! No-bod-y home, Meat nor drink nor mon-ey have I none, Yet will I be mer - ry.—

Suggestion:
To finish the song, continue repeating Part 1 until the last group joins in.

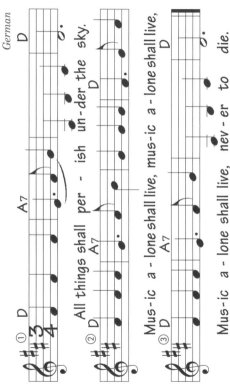

MUSIC ALONE SHALL LIVE

German

All things shall per - ish un-der the sky.

Mus-ic a - lone shall live, mus-ic a - lone shall live,

Mus-ic a - lone shall live, nev - er - to die.

17

LET US SING TOGETHER

Czechoslovakia

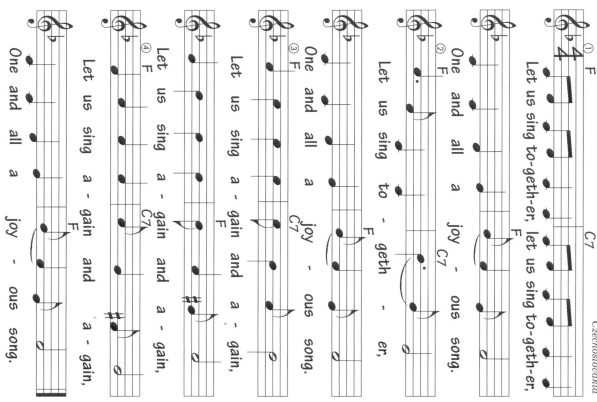

Let us sing to-geth-er, let us sing to-geth-er,

One and all a joy - ous song.

Let us sing to - geth - er,

One and all a joy - ous song.

Let us sing a - gain and a - gain,

Let us sing a - gain and a - gain,

Let us sing a - gain and a - gain,

One and all a joy - ous song.

Day Is Done

HE'S GOT THE WHOLE WORLD

Spiritual

1. He's got the whole world__ in His hands,__ He's got the
whole world__ in His hands,__ He's got the whole world__
in His hands,__ He's got the whole world in His hands.

2. He's got the little, bitty baby in His hands,
He's got the little, bitty baby in His hands,
He's got the little, bitty baby in His hands,
He's got the whole world in His hands.

3. He's got you and me, brother …

4. He's got you and me, sister …

5. He's got everybody here …

6. He's got the wind and the rain …

7. He's got the sun and the moon …

8. He's got the whole world …

Suggestion: (for two-part song)
Sing with *Rocka My Soul* (page 31).

20

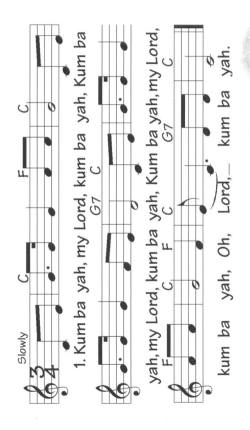

Slowly

3/4

C   F   C

1. Kum ba yah, my Lord, kum ba yah, Kum ba

G7   C

yah, my Lord, kum ba yah, Kum ba yah, my Lord,

F   C   G7   C

kum ba   yah,   Oh,   Lord,___   kum ba   yah.

2. Someone's crying, Lord, kum ba yah,
   Someone's crying, Lord, kum ba yah,
   Someone's crying, Lord, kum ba yah,
   Oh, Lord, kum ba yah.

3. Someone's laughing, Lord . . .

4. Someone's singing, Lord . . .

5. Someone's praying, Lord . . .

6. Kum ba yah, my Lord . . .

Translation: Come by here

Action:
- *kum ba*—roll hands
- *yah*—hands outstretched
- *my*—point to self
- *Lord*—point upward

21

TELL ME WHY

Traditional

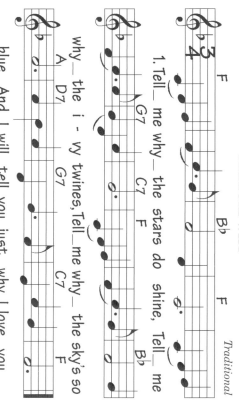

F   B♭   F

1. Tell__ me why__ the stars do shine, Tell__ me

      G7   C7   F   B♭

why__ the i - vy twines, Tell__ me why__ the sky's so

A   D7   G7   C7   F

blue, And I will tell you just why I love you.

2. Because God made the stars to shine,
Because God made the ivy twine,
Because God made the sky so blue,
Because God made you, that's why I love you.

22

MICHAEL, ROW THE BOAT ASHORE

Spiritual

1. Mi-chael, row the boat a - shore, Hal-le - lu - jah,

Mi-chael, row the boat a - shore, Hal-le-lu - jah.

2. Sister, help to trim the sails, Hallelujah,
   Sister, help to trim the sails, Hallelujah.

3. The river is deep and the river is wide …
   Milk and honey on the other side …

4. Jordan's river is chilly and cold …
   Chills the body but warms the soul …

5. Michael, row the boat ashore …

DOWN IN THE VALLEY

Kentucky

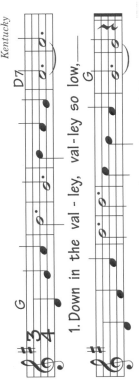

1. Down in the val - ley, val - ley so low,

Hang your head o - ver, hear the wind blow.

2. Hear the wind blow, Dear, hear the wind blow,
   Hang your head over, hear the wind blow.

3. Roses love sunshine, violets love dew,
   Angels in heaven know I love you.

4. Know I love you, Dear, know I love you,
   Angels in heaven know I love you.

23

OH, SHENANDOAH

American Chantey, 1800s

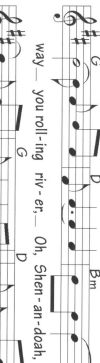

1. Oh, Shen-an-doah, I long to hear you, A-way — you roll-ing riv-er, Oh, Shen-an-doah, I long to hear you, A - way, I'm bound a- way, 'Cross the wide Mis - sou - ri.

2. Oh, Shenandoah, I love your daughter,
Away, you rolling river;
I'll take her 'cross the rolling water,
Away, we're bound away,
'Cross the wide Missouri.

3. Oh, Shenandoah, I'm bound to leave you …
Oh, Shenandoah, I'll not deceive you …

I KNOW WHERE I'M GOIN'

Irish

1. I know where I'm go-in', And I know who's go-in' with me,— I know who I love,— But the dear knows who I'll mar-ry.—

2. I have stockings of silk
And shoes of fine green leather,
Combs to buckle my hair,
And a ring for every finger.

3. Feather beds are soft
And painted rooms are bonny,
But I would trade them all
For my handsome, winsome Johnny.

(Repeat verse 1)

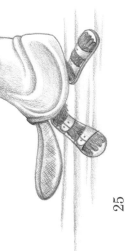

THE RIDDLE SONG

Appalachian

1.I gave my love a cher-ry that has no stone,I
gave my love a chick-en that has no bone, I
gave my love a sto-ry that has no end, I
gave my love a ba-by with no cry - in.'

2. How can there be a cherry that has no stone?
How can there be a chicken that has no bone?
How can there be a story that has no end?
How can there be a baby with no cryin'?

3. A cherry when it's bloomin', it has no stone,
A chicken when it's pippin*, it has no bone,
The story that I love you, it has no end,
A baby when it's sleepin', there's no cryin'.

*pippin: in the shell

26

WAYFARING STRANGER

Kentucky, 1801

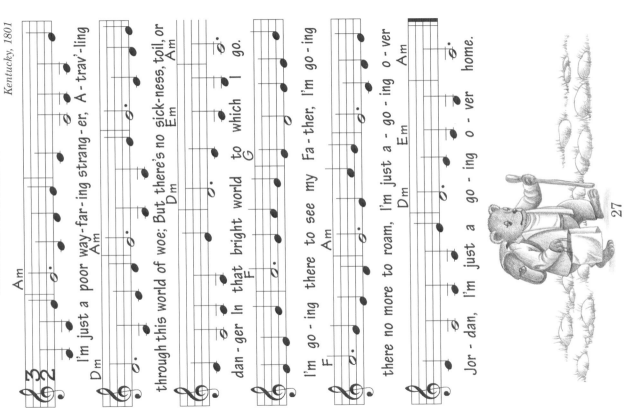

I'm just a poor way-far-ing strang-er, A-trav'-ling through this world of woe; But there's no sick-ness, toil, or dan-ger In that bright world to which I go.

I'm go-ing there to see my Fa-ther, I'm go-ing there no more to roam, I'm just a-go-ing o-ver Jor-dan, I'm just a go-ing o-ver home.

27

I LOVE THE MOUNTAINS

(Round)

Traditional

F   Dm

Boom - de - ah - da,   boom - de - ah - da,

Gm   C7

Boom - de - ah - da,   boom - de - ah - da,

① F   Dm   Gm   C7

I love the moun-tains, I love the roll-ing hills,

② F   Dm   Gm   C7

I love the flow - ers,   I love the daf-fo-dils,

③ F   Dm   Gm   C7

I love the fire - side When all the lights are low.

Chorus/Repeat until all parts join in

F   Dm

Boom-de-ah-da, boom-de-ah-da, Boom-de-

Ending

F   C7   F

Gm   C7

ah - da, boom - de - ay,   Boom, boom, boom.

28

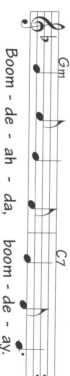

SING YOUR WAY HOME

Traditional

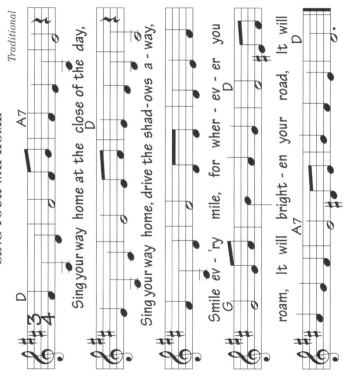

Sing your way home at the close of the day,
Sing your way home, drive the shad-ows a-way,
Smile ev-'ry mile, for wher-ev-er you
roam, It will bright-en your road, It will
light-en your load, If you sing your way home.

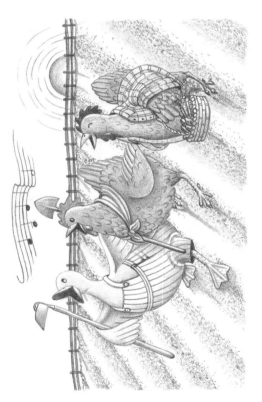

29

EV'RY NIGHT WHEN THE SUN GOES IN

Appalachian

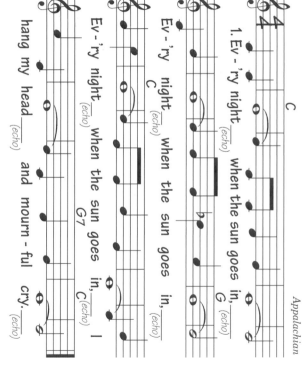

1. Ev - 'ry night   when the sun goes in, *(echo)*

Ev - 'ry night *(echo)* when the sun goes in, *(echo)*

Ev - 'ry night *(echo)* when the sun goes in, *(echo)*

hang my head *(echo)* and mourn - ful cry. *(echo)*

2. If the stars (echo) in the sky won't shine, ...
   If the stars ... in the sky won't shine, ...
   If the stars ... in the sky won't shine, ...
   I hang my head ... and mournful cry. ...

3. If the moon ... hides behind a cloud ...

Suggestion:
Sing with two groups, the second echoing where shown.

30